This Book Belongs To

Made in the USA
Monee, IL
24 September 2022

14570648R00059